Inside

Mary Elizabeth's House

For Julie Watts

Viking
Penguin Books Australia Ltd
487 Maroondah Highway, PO Box 257
Ringwood, Victoria 3134, Australia
Penguin Books Ltd
Harmondsworth, Middlesex, England
Penguin Putnam Inc.
375 Hudson Street, New York, New York 10014, USA
Penguin Books Canada Limited
10 Alcorn Avenue, Toronto, Ontario, Canada, M4V 3B2
Penguin Books (N.Z.) Ltd
Cnr Rosedale and Airborne Roads, Albany, Auckland, New Zealand
Penguin Books (South Africa) (Pty) Ltd
5 Watkins Street, Denver Ext 4, 2094, South Africa
Penguin Books India (P) Ltd
11, Community Centre, Panchsheel Park, New Delhi – 110 017, India

First published by Penguin Books Australia, 2000

1 3 5 7 9 10 8 6 4 2

Copyright © Pamela Allen, 2000

Designed by Deborah Brash/Brash Design Pty Ltd, Sydney
Typeset in 24pt Stone Serif by Brash Design Pty Ltd
printed and bound by South China Co. Ltd/Hong Kong/China

National Library of Australia
Cataloguing-in-Publication data:

Allen, Pamela, 1934- .
Inside Mary Elizabeth's house.

ISBN 0 670 89133 9.

1. Title.

A823.3

www.puffin.com.au

Inside
Mary Elizabeth's House

Pamela Allen

VIKING

Here is Mary Elizabeth's house.

This is Mary Elizabeth,

and these are the boys.

On Monday morning,
on the way to school,
Mary Elizabeth
said to the boys,

'There's a monster at my house.'

'We don't believe you!' they said.

'They don't believe me,' she said.

On Tuesday morning
Mary Elizabeth said to the boys,
'There's a monster at my house
with red blood-shot eyes
and sharp pointy teeth.

He's rough and he's rowdy
and he jumps on my bed.'

'We *don't* believe you,' they said.

'They *won't* believe me,' she said.

'Huh! Huh! Ugh!'

On Wednesday morning
Mary Elizabeth said to the boys,
'There's a monster at my house
with red blood-shot eyes
and sharp pointy teeth.

He's rough and he's rowdy
and jumps on my bed.
He doesn't wash and
he won't clean his teeth.

My mother says that he'll have to go
but he likes it at my house,
he told me so.'

'We don't BELIEVE you!' they cried.
And they laughed.

'They STILL won't believe me,' she said.

'Huh! Huh! Ugh! Huh! Ugh! Ugh!'

On Thursday morning
on the way to school,
Mary Elizabeth said to the boys,
'There IS a monster at my house.'

'We don't believe you,
we don't believe you,
we don't believe you,'
they chanted.

Mary Elizabeth smiled.
'I'll show you,' she said.
'Come for dinner tonight at seven.'
'Yum! FOOD!' the boys shouted.

'It's the house painted red.
Number eleven.
You'll see,' said Mary Elizabeth.

Later that night,
about a quarter to seven,
the boys set out for number eleven.

'She did say number eleven, didn't she?'

Knock! Knock! Knock!

It was seven o'clock.

Mary Elizabeth came to the door.

'We're here and we're hungry,' the boys cried.
'What's for dinner?'
Slowly Mary Elizabeth smiled her sweet smile.
'Come in,' she said, 'and see . . .'

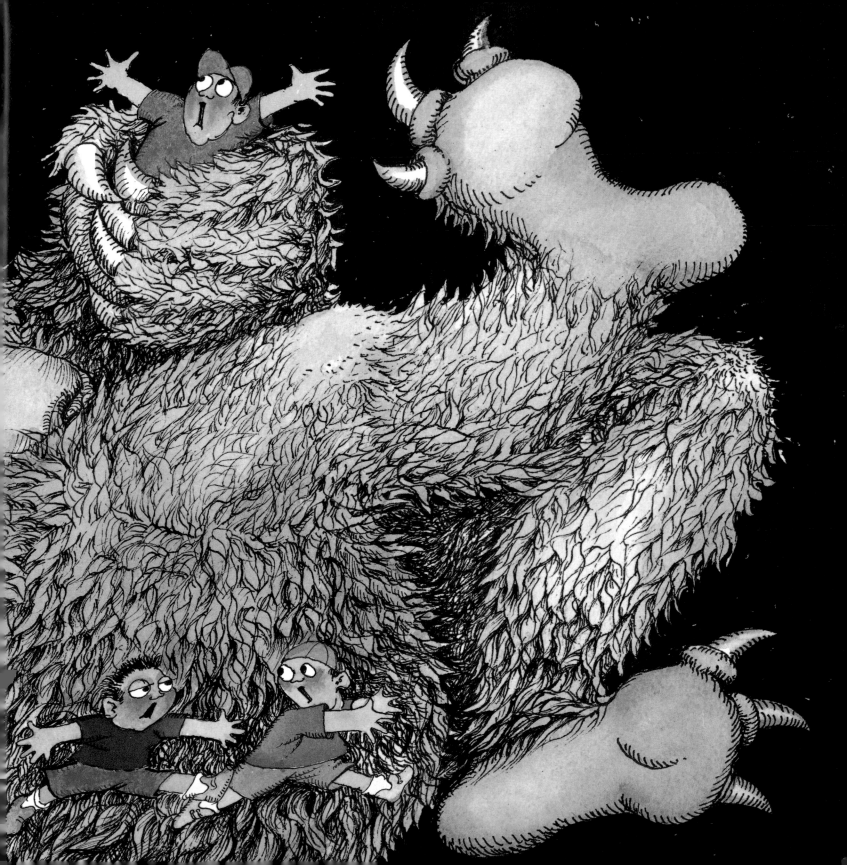

'YAAAAAAAAAA

AAAAHHHHH!'

'Now they believe me,' she said.